CALUMET CITY PUBLIC LIBRARY
3 1613 00361 8611
P9-DHQ-659

Lynn Reiser

Hardworking Puppies

Harcourt, Inc.

Orlando Austin New York San Diego Toronto London

www.HarcourtBooks.com

Library of Congress Cataloging-in-Publication Data
Reiser, Lynn.
Hardworking puppies/Lynn Reiser.
p. cm.
Summary: One by one, ten energetic puppies find important jobs as dogs who help people in different ways, including by pulling sleds and saving swimmers.
[1. Working dogs—Fiction. 2. Dogs—Fiction. 3. Subtraction—Fiction.] I. Title.
PZ7.R27745Har 2006
[E]—dc22 2004021505
ISBN-13: 978-0152-05404-5 ISBN-10: 0-15-205404-9

C E G H F D B

Printed in Singapore

The illustrations in this book were created with Sharpie markers, Wite-Out, watercolor paint, scissors, tape, and a copy machine.

The display and text type were set in Opti Bernhard Gothic.
Color separations by Colourscan Co. Pte. Ltd., Singapore
Printed and bound by Tien Wah Press, Singapore
This book was printed on totally chlorine-free Stora Enso Matte paper.
Production supervision by Pascha Gerlinger
Designed by Scott Piehl and Lauren Rille

**For working dogs
and their people**

Once there were ten hardworking puppies. The puppies worked hard keeping busy.

But one day,
just keeping busy was not enough.
The puppies wanted more.

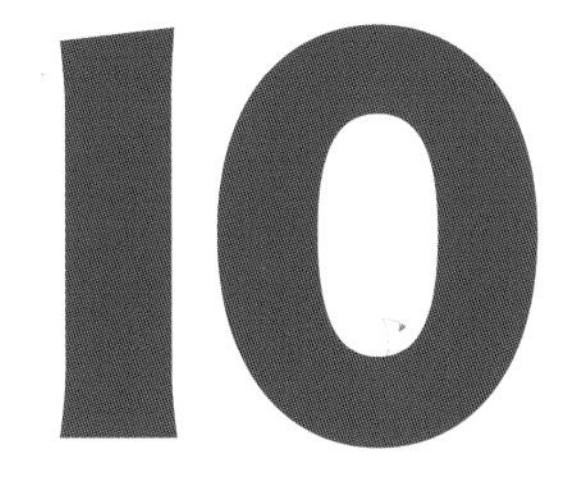

The TEN puppies all wanted jobs!

**Along came a firefighter.
The firefighter needed a hardworking puppy.**

TEN puppies wanting jobs
minus
ONE beginner firefighter puppy
equals...

NINE puppies
all wanting jobs!

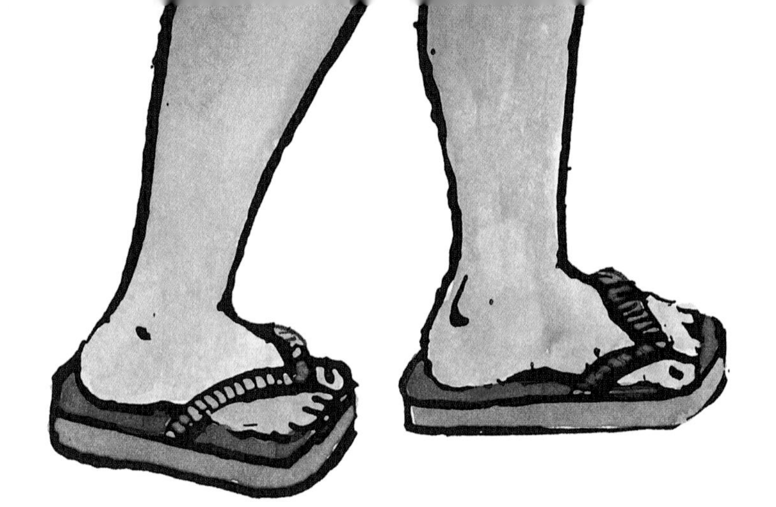

Along came a lifeguard.
The lifeguard needed a hardworking puppy.

NINE puppies wanting jobs
minus
ONE junior water-rescue puppy
equals...

EIGHT puppies all wanting jobs!

Along came a clown.
The clown needed a hardworking puppy.

EIGHT puppies wanting jobs
minus
ONE assistant clown puppy
equals...

7

SEVEN puppies
all wanting jobs!

Along came a photographer.
The photographer needed a hardworking puppy.

SEVEN puppies wanting jobs
minus
ONE debut model puppy
equals...

6

SIX puppies all wanting jobs!

Along came a sled driver.
The sled driver needed a hardworking puppy.

SIX puppies wanting jobs
minus
ONE apprentice sled puppy
equals...

FIVE puppies all wanting jobs!

Along came a hospital volunteer. The volunteer needed a hardworking puppy.

FIVE puppies wanting jobs
minus
ONE student therapy puppy
equals...

4

FOUR puppies
all wanting jobs!

Along came an airport security officer.
The officer needed a hardworking puppy.

FOUR puppies wanting jobs
minus
ONE rookie airport security puppy
equals...

3

THREE puppies
all wanting jobs!

**Along came a groundskeeper.
The groundskeeper needed a hardworking puppy.**

THREE puppies wanting jobs
minus
ONE novice herding puppy
equals...

TWO puppies
both tired of waiting!

Along came a guide-dog instructor.
The instructor needed a hardworking puppy.

TWO puppies tired of waiting
minus
ONE guide puppy in training
equals...

1

ONE lonely puppy still wanting a job.

Then, along came a boy.
The boy needed a hardworking puppy.

The last puppy became an expert pet.

**After that,
all ten puppies kept busy working hard,
and when their work was done . . .**

...THEY PLAYED!

PAW NOTES

All puppies grow up to be dogs. Some lucky puppies grow up to be dogs with jobs. There are so many jobs that dogs can do.

GUARD DOGS protect property and homes. Police dogs ride in squad cars or patrol the streets with K9 officers. Dalmatians watch over firehouses when the firefighters are responding to an alarm.

WATER-RESCUE DOGS save swimmers in trouble. Years ago dogs herded fish, hauled in nets, dove for lost objects, and carried messages between boats. Today, Portuguese Water Dogs retrieve fish and game—and sometimes home-run baseballs from the San Francisco Bay!

PERFORMING DOGS pose for photos, act in circuses, and appear in movies and television shows. Some become famous and enjoy luxuries like dog massages and room service in hotels.

SLED DOG TEAMS deliver food and medical supplies to snowbound villages. The lead dog can find its way through blizzards when the musher can no longer see the trail. Sled dog teams also race for sport.

THERAPY DOGS comfort and amuse patients in hospitals and nursing homes. These dogs wear official jackets and ID badges just like other caregivers.

AIRPORT SECURITY DOGS sniff luggage to find illegal cargo. The expert noses in the U.S. Department of Agriculture's Beagle Brigade can recognize over fifty different smells. Search and rescue dogs look for lost people and pets. They also help locate victims of fires, earthquakes, and other disasters.

HERDING DOGS tend cattle and sheep. They also round up Canada geese to keep the big birds away from crowded parks, playgrounds, golf courses, and airports.

ASSISTANCE DOGS help their human partners by pulling wheelchairs, opening doors, turning light switches on and off, and picking up dropped objects. Signal dogs alert their hearing-impaired owners to sounds like the doorbell buzzing, the telephone ringing, or a baby crying. Guide dogs go everywhere with their masters. They are trained to ignore friendly pats or food from strangers.

Even **PET DOGS** have work to do. They strive to be gentle, obedient, and patient companions. And sometimes they go to school to learn to do their job better.

These are only a few of the jobs dogs can do.
But no matter what their duties,
hardworking dogs everywhere are happy
to be paid in food, shelter, treats—
and love.

HARDWORKING NUMBERS

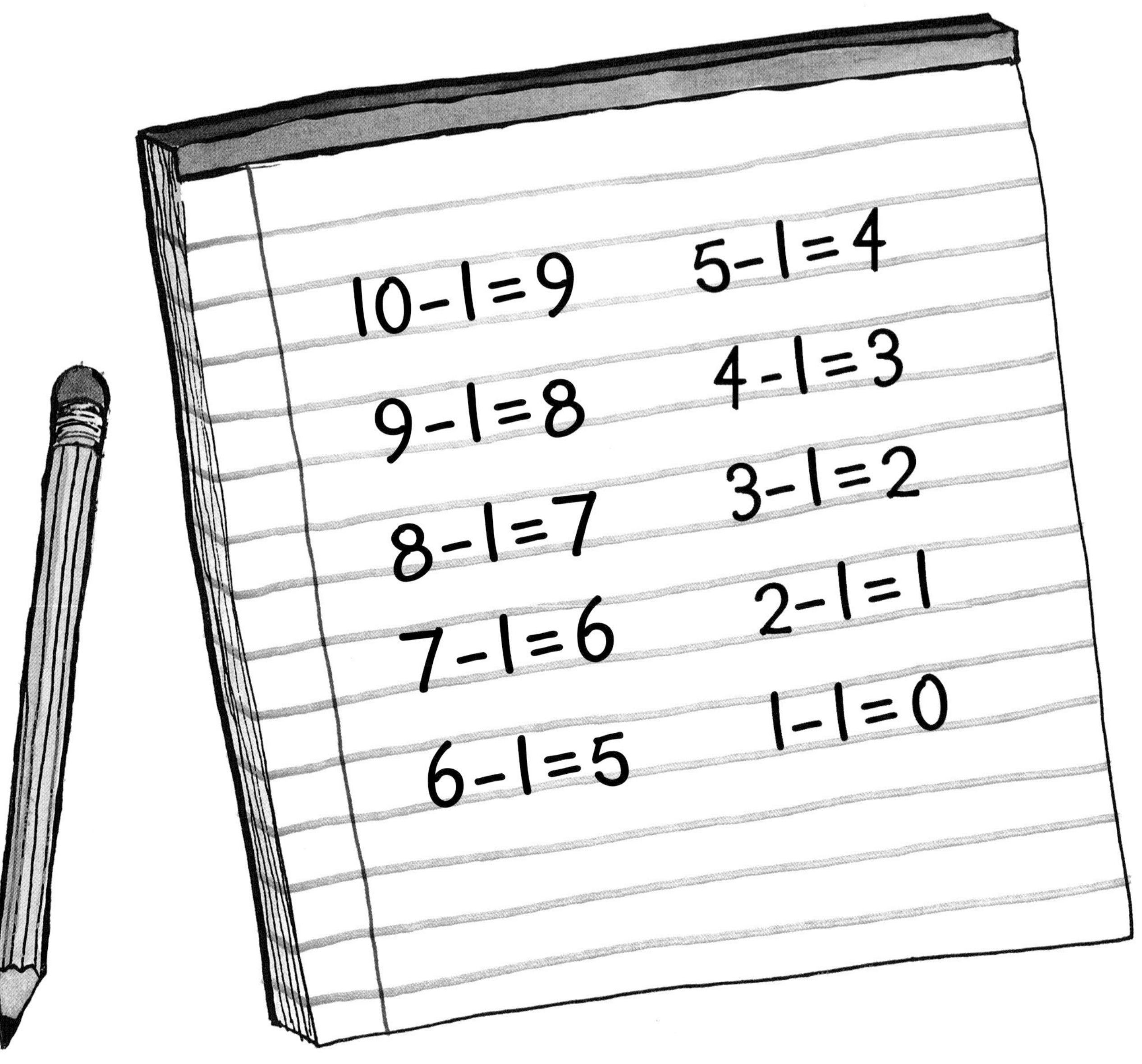